WEIRD SEA CREATURES™
THE STINGRAY

Miriam J. Gross

The Rosen Publishing Group's
PowerKids Press™
New York

For Aunt Ilona

Published in 2006 by The Rosen Publishing Group, Inc.
29 East 21st Street, New York, NY 10010

First Edition

Editor: Daryl Heller
Book Design: Albert B. Hanner
Book Layout: Gregory Tucker

Photo Credits: Cover © Jeff Rotman/SeaPics.com; p. 5 © Masa Ushioda/SeaPics.com; pp. 6, 9, 10 © Doug Perrine/SeaPics.com; p. 13 © Mark Conlin/SeaPics.com; p. 14 © Ingrid Visser/SeaPics.com; p. 17 © Jeff Jaskolski/SeaPics.com; p. 18 © James D. Watt/SeaPics.com; p. 21 © Philippe Colombi/Getty Images.

Library of Congress Cataloging-in-Publication Data

Gross, Miriam J.
The stingray / Miriam J. Gross.
p. cm. — (Weird sea creatures)
Includes index.
ISBN 1-4042-3190-0 (library binding)
1. Stingrays—Juvenile literature. I. Title. II. Series: Gross, Miriam J. Weird sea creatures.

QL638.8G76 2006
597.3'5—dc22

2004029410

Manufactured in the United States of America

CONTENTS

Is It a Fish or a Pancake?

A stingray often rests in the sand on the ocean floor. The eyes of a stingray stick out from the top of its body and allow this creature to see any approaching danger. However, most animals will not notice this weird, flat animal. Shaped like a pancake, this sand-colored creature blends in with, or matches, the ocean floor. Should anything come along to bother it, a stingray can strike with a whiplike tail that is armed with **venomous spines**.

Stingrays and other types of rays, such as manta rays and electric rays, are related to sharks. In fact some scientists call them pancake sharks. Both sharks and rays are part of a group that scientists call Chondrichthyes, or cartilaginous fish. Instead of having **skeletons** made of hard bone, these fish have skeletons made of softer cartilage. Cartilage is the same matter from which human ears and noses are made.

This southern stingray is in Biscayne National Park in Miami, Florida. Biscayne is the largest marine, or ocean, park in the United States. The stingray is shown on a bed of sea grass, a type of grass that grows in salt water. Clams, which stingrays eat, are often found in sea grass beds.

eye

spiracle

One of this blue-spotted ribbontail ray's two spiracles can be seen behind the creature's eye. Spiracles are openings in the stingray's body that allow water, which holds oxygen, to enter the creature's body. The oxygen is later separated from the water when it moves through the stingray's gills.

STINGRAY BASICS

Most fish have fins that are thin and **flexible**. The fins of stingrays, however, are thick and stiff. The wide pectoral, or side, fins of rays are completely joined to the body and form a disc around it.

In some **species**, such as the yellow stingray, the disc is round, giving the stingray the shape of a frying pan. The southern stingray has fins that are pointed at the sides, which gives this ray the shape of a kite. Stingrays swim by waving the edges of these fins.

Stingrays breathe through gills, as do all fish. Gills are organs, or body parts, that gather oxygen from the water and send it to the animal's bloodstream. Stingrays take in water through their mouths and through openings behind the eyes called spiracles. Water leaves a stingray's body through gill **slits** on the underside of its body.

Scales cover the skin of most fish. Scales are tiny plates that fit together over the skin to protect it. The skin of rays and sharks is covered with small scales that hold a tiny tooth called a dermal denticle. The dermal denticle makes the ray's skin rough if it is rubbed in the wrong direction.

SO MANY SENSES

In addition to good eyesight and a fine sense of smell, stingrays have a sharp sense of hearing and touch. A stingray's ears are tiny openings on top of its head. Hairlike cells in the **inner** ear detect, or sense, sound **vibrations**. These vibrations send a nerve signal, or message, to the brain. Similar cells are found on the outside of the stingray's body and give the creature its sense of touch. Stingrays can even sense objects that are sitting still, by the way water currents bounce off the motionless object.

Stingrays also possess electrosense. All living animals have a weak electrical field of **energy** around their bodies. This is caused by electrical activity in muscles, as well as electrical charges in body fluids, or liquids, such as blood.

A stingray's special electrosense helps it hunt for clams, shrimp, worms, and sea stars under the sand. The stingray can sense the weak electrical signal given off by these hidden creatures.

This southern stingray is using electrosense to find prey that lies hidden in the sand. When an animal bleeds from a wound, it increases the amount of electrical energy that flows into the water around it. This flow makes wounded animals an easy catch for animals that use electrosense.

A blue-spotted ribbontail stingray was found in a coral reef that is part of Layang-Layang Atoll in Malaysia. An atoll is a coral reef that forms a small island in a shallow, or not too deep, body of water. A coral reef has many bright colors, including blue, which allow animals such as this stingray to blend in with their surroundings.

HOME SWEET HOME

Stingrays are found all over the world in many different **habitats**. Most species live in the warm, **shallow** coastal waters of **tropical** oceans. Other species, such as the sixgill stingray, live deeper in the open sea. The blue-spotted ribbontail ray is found in **coral reefs**.

Stingrays do not have regular homes. These animals have **evolved** a body shape that is ideal for living on the floor of the ocean. Their flat bodies allow them to rest in the sand or mud and bury themselves to hide from **predators**. The stingray's mouth is on the underside of its body, which makes it easier for them to eat the food found in the sand below them.

Most stingrays are brownish or greenish in color to blend in with the sand or mud. Stingrays that live in coral reefs can be brighter in color because their habitats are more colorful.

Stingrays are often bothered by worms and leeches that live on a stingray's skin and make it sick. To get rid of these pests, stingrays visit "cleaning stations." At a cleaning station, smaller fish, such as wrasses, will gather around the stingray and eat the pests. This helps stingrays stay clean and healthy.

11

DINING IN THE SAND

Stingrays are always growing new teeth. New sets of teeth form in rows behind the old ones. The new teeth move forward as the old ones fall out. A stingray never has to go very long with broken or worn-down teeth.

Stingrays are carnivores, which means that they eat meat. They **especially** like shrimp and clams that live in the sand of the ocean floor. The stingray uses its sense of smell and electrosense to locate these animals. They do not use their eyes to hunt. A stingray's eyes are on top of its body, so it cannot see below itself, which is where its food is found.

To catch its **prey**, a stingray traps the animal against the ground with its body. Then it uses its body to roll the prey toward its mouth. The stingray has rows of strong teeth that it uses to crush, or smash, the shells of its prey to get at the meat that is inside the shell.

Stingrays have evolved to live for long periods of time without eating. One way they do this is by lying still on the seafloor, which uses little energy. Their bodies also **digest** food slowly, so they do not have to eat very often.

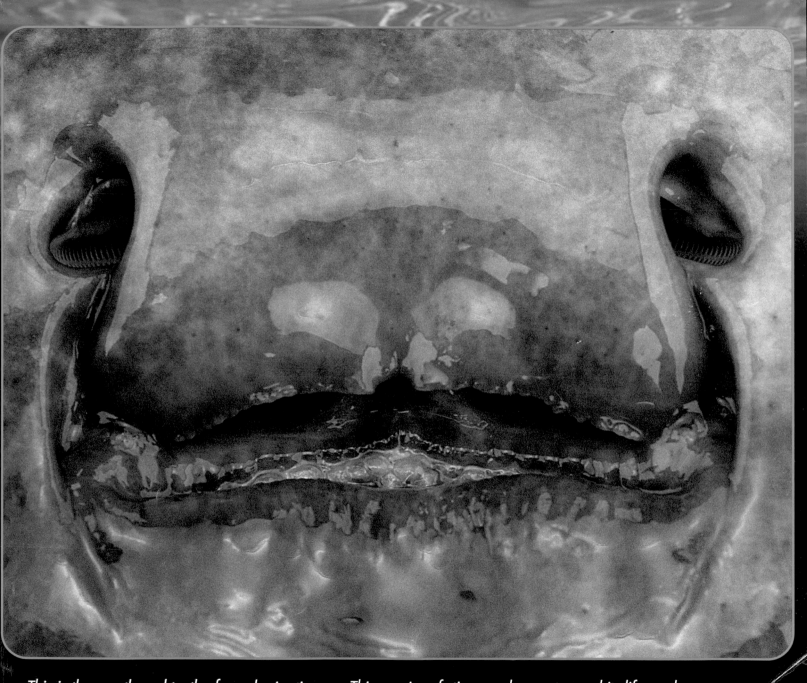

This is the mouth and teeth of a pelagic stingray. This species of stingray does not spend its life on the ocean floor. Instead it hunts and swims in deep ocean waters. Nature has given the pelagic stingray some teeth that have sharp edges. These sharp edges allow the pelagic stingray to cut meat. This is useful when it feeds on animals such as herring and octopus.

Orcas are meat eaters that sometimes feed on stingrays. Orcas often hunt in groups. Scientists have witnessed an orca catching a stingray in its mouth and then tossing the stingray to another orca. This may be a method of killing a stingray, or it may be how adult orcas teach their young to hunt.

PREDATORS

Stingrays are a favorite food of large sharks, crocodiles, orcas, and birds that fly along the water's surface. To hide from predators, stingrays often bury themselves in the sand. To do this they flap, or beat, their fins and stir up the sand until it covers them. Unfortunately, this does not keep them safe from the hammerhead shark, which uses its own electrosense to find the stingray.

The stingray's main **defense** against attacks from predators is on its tail. A sharp spine with venom **glands** lines the base of a stingray's tail, which can be 9 feet (2.7 m) long in some species.

If a stingray is in danger, it will arch, or curve, its back, snap its tail, and then drive its spine into the attacker. This poisonous spine is often called a stinger. The venom in the glands makes the wound very painful. People rarely die from a stingray's venom. However, the wound should be checked by a doctor to make sure that it does not become **infected**.

MATING AND THE LIFE CYCLE

Male and female stingrays come together in late winter and spring to **mate**. Males search for females who are ready to mate using their sense of smell and electrosense. Females give out scent signals to attract, or draw, these males.

Most fish spawn, which means they lay eggs that are **fertilized** in the water. In stingrays, however, the eggs are fertilized and carried inside the female until they are ready to be born. The mother may carry from 2 to 10 babies inside her body for two to four months. Baby stingrays, which are called pups, are born with spines on their tails.

Because the pups have had time to grow inside their mothers, they are large enough to feed themselves and to fight off predators at birth. Stingrays grow slowly, and some may not produce offspring until they are 10 or 11 years old.

A male stingray is shown courting a female stingray. The female stingray is somewhat covered with sand. If a female stingray is not interested in mating with a male, she may try to fight him off with her stinger.

These southern stingrays are swimming in the Caribbean Sea at Stingray City, an area of the Cayman Islands in the West Indies. About 30 stingrays return daily to Stingray City to be fed by visitors and locals. Because people have been feeding these stingrays for so many years, they have become tame.

TWO SPECIES OF STINGRAYS

There are about 70 known species of stingrays around the world. The southern stingray is the species that is most often seen by divers who **explore** the coral reefs in Florida, the Bahamas, the Gulf of Mexico, and the Caribbean. The southern stingray is diamond shaped and can grow to 6.6 feet (2 m) wide. These stingrays are usually grey, olive green, or brown on top. They are white underneath.

The blue-spotted ribbontail ray lives in warm shallow waters from South Africa to the Solomon Islands in the South Pacific. This species is about 1 foot (.3 m) wide. It is often found in coral reefs, such as Australia's Great Barrier Reef, where it can hide under coral and in caves. This blue-spotted ribbontail ray has a tan or yellowish green background patterned with bright blue polka dots. Two bright blue stripes run down the tail, and a fold of flesh on the tail looks like a fan. The stomach of this stingray is white.

STINGRAYS IN DANGER

Many sea creatures lay thousands of eggs at a time to make sure that enough of the eggs last to adulthood. Stingrays have only a few babies at a time. Therefore, they can become **endangered** if the babies are killed in large numbers. Nature cannot replace, or bring back, the population quickly enough to keep the species alive.

Stingrays are often hunted for the spines, or stingers, on their tails, which are used to make **weapons** and gems. People also make leather and some kinds of sandpaper from stingray skin.

Fishermen sometimes kill stingrays when trying to catch other fish. Trawl nets, which sweep, or brush, the ocean floor for shrimp, often catch more rays than they do shrimp. These nets also flatten the seafloor and destroy the habitats and hiding places of the animals on which stingrays feed. Some **freshwater** species of stingrays have been poisoned when their river habitats become polluted.

This shrimp fisherman has pulled up his nets from the water to see what he has caught. Unfortunately, stingrays are sometimes brought up in these nets, too.

MEETING PEOPLE

Since stingrays often lie hidden in the sand, people **wading** in shallow waters sometimes accidentally step on them. The frightened stingray reacts by driving its stinger into the wader's foot or leg. Although the wound caused by a stingray is painful, it is hardly ever deadly.

A good way to avoid stepping on stingrays is to shuffle your feet as you walk in shallow waters. These movements warn stingrays that you are there. The stingrays will probably swim away.

Stingrays will not usually try to harm people. In fact there are many places where people can go to swim with stingrays. One such place is Stingray City in the Cayman Islands in the West Indies. The stingrays are curious about the divers, and the divers can see up close how beautiful and gentle the stingrays are. It is to be hoped that these meetings will make people more concerned about protecting these unusual animals and their habitats.

GLOSSARY

coral reefs (KOR-ul REEFS) Underwater hills of coral.

defense (dih-FENS) A feature of a living thing that helps to protect it.

digest (dy-JEST) To break down food so that the body can use it.

endangered (en-DAYN-jerd) In danger of no longer existing.

energy (EH-nur-jee) The power to work or to act.

especially (is-PESH-lee) Mainly.

evolved (ih-VOLVD) Changed over many years.

explore (ek-SPLOR) To go over carefully or examine.

fertilized (FUR-tuh-lyzd) Added male cells to a female's egg to make babies.

flexible (FLEK-sih-bul) Being able to move and bend in many ways.

freshwater (FRESH-wah-ter) Having to do with water without salt.

glands (GLANDZ) Parts of the body that produce an element to help with a bodily function.

habitats (HA-bih-tats) The surroundings where animals or plants naturally live.

infected (in-FEK-tid) Given a sickness that is caused by germs.

inner (IH-ner) Further inside or within.

mate (MAYT) To join together to make babies.

predators (PREH-duh-terz) Animals that kill other animals for food.

prey (PRAY) An animal that is hunted by another animal for food.

shallow (SHA-loh) Not deep.

skeletons (SKEH-lih-tunz) The bones in an animal's or a person's body.

slits (SLITS) Straight, narrow cuts, tears, or openings.

species (SPEE-sheez) A single kind of living thing. All people are one species.

spines (SPYNZ) Hard, pointed edges on a stingray's tail that are often called stingers.

tropical (TRAH-puh-kul) Having to do with a part of Earth that is near the equator. It is always warm in the tropics.

venomous (VEH-nuh-mis) Having a poisonous bite or sting.

vibrations (vy-BRAY-shunz) Fast movements up and down or back and forth.

wading (WAYD-ing) Walking or swimming in shallow water.

weapons (WEH-punz) Objects or tools used to injure, disable, or kill.

INDEX

WEB SITES

Due to the changing nature of Internet links, PowerKids Press has developed an online list of Web sites related to the subject of this book. This site is updated regularly. Please use this link to access the list:
www.powerkidslinks.com/wsc/stingray/